ST.
ON THE
LINE

CW00409582

STAY ON THE LINE

CLAY McLEOD CHAPMAN

ILLUSTRATIONS BY
TREVOR HENDERSON

 SHORTWAVE
PUBLISHING

Shortwave Publishing
contact@shortwavepublishing.com
Full Catalog: shortwavepublishing.com

Stay on the Line is a work of fiction. The characters, incidents, and dialogue are creations of the author's imagination or are used fictitiously. Any resemblance to actual events or persons, living or dead, is entirely coincidental.

Copyright © 2024 by Clay McLeod Chapman

All rights reserved.

Cover art and illustrations by Trevor Henderson.

Cover design and interior layout by Alan Lastufka.

First Edition published July 2024.

10 9 8 7 6 5 4 3 2 1

ISBN 978-1-959565-32-1 (paperback)
ISBN 978-1-959565-33-8 (ebook)

For Indrani

STAY
ON THE
LINE

Seems cruel that Aubrey took everything but the phone booth. Of all the things Brandywine had to offer that goddamn hurricane, you'd think a disconnected payphone was ripe for the picking. Ma Bell had cut service ages ago, rendering it dead, but nobody from AT&T ever got around to removing the booth. They just left it there in the parking lot, a freestanding shack of cracked glass overlooking the marina, not doing anybody a lick of good. The rusted insides were covered in all kinds of graffiti, a kudzu of scribbles and dicks that only grew thicker throughout the years. Kids never even had a clue what a payphone was, what it was once used for, well before their hormones kicked in and turned it into an impromptu kissing booth. I was always catching young couples making out inside it nearly every night, looking like yet another pair of Japanese fighting fish crammed into an aquarium. Never had the heart to kick them out.

Let 'em peck, I thought. At least the booth was still good for something.

You kissed me in there plenty of times. How many tipsy nights ended with the two of us slipping into the booth, sealing ourselves in, pressing our backs against the glass and diving in?

It should've been the booth that got swept away.

Not you.

Shelby always thought it was the tiniest lighthouse. Still does. I remember one night listening to you spin this yarn as you tucked her into bed, talking about the booth as if it was a long-extinct beast. Just another one of your handmade fairy tales, this one about some mythical unicorn of telecommunication. "Once upon a time," you started in like you always started, "a long, long while ago, long before there were cell phones or Wi-Fi, your mommy and daddy had to chat using these big ol' phones rooted to the ground. We all called them *landlines*."

"What's a landline?" Shelby asked.

"Well. . . they were like trees growing out from the earth, connected together by miles of wires. Everybody had one in their house. Some still do. But a phone booth didn't belong to anybody. It was for *everyone.* You'd step into that glass cubby and close the door, sealing yourself in, pick the phone up and bring it to your ear, drop a quarter in, then dial. You couldn't move around. Couldn't wander away. You had to stay put. All you could do was just... *talk.*"

Shelby still didn't believe you, all four years of herself. "*Nuh-huh,* you're lying..."

"Hand to God, that's what they were used for."

"You mean I can call anybody I want?"

"Well... Not anymore."

"Why not?"

"'Cause it doesn't work now, sugar. The phone's been turned off. Wires have been cut."

"Then why's it still out there?"

"To remind us how things used to be, I reckon. How far we've come."

"Go ahead and tell her what people use it for now," I teased. "I dare you."

You gave me that devilish grin of yours. Or maybe it was sheepish. Hard to say with your whiskers covering your lips, but I swear I saw you blush from under your beard.

"What's Mom talking about?" Shelby asked, completely clueless to her own conception.

"Yeah," I said, "why don't you tell Shelby what Mommy's talking about."

"We'll save that story for another night, hon..."

We could never afford childcare. That meant one of us had to look after Shelby while the other was on the clock. I wasn't about to let her hop on your trawler and spend the whole morning hauling in herring with you, so that meant most days she was stuck with me at the bar.

I've been bartending at Braddock's for longer than I want to admit. The owners live all the way in Pungo, so the bar might as well be mine. We've always had the best view of the bay. The marina up front is full of commercial fishermen, clotting up the docks with their deadrises.

It's where I met you, now, wasn't it? Still remember it as if it were yesterday. How many moons ago was that? How many hurricanes have we weathered together? You'd just come in with your fishing buds after wrestling against the Chesapeake all day. You all reeked of dead halibut, plopping your asses down, and I thought, *Fishermen never die, they just smell that way.*

You had to buy the first round, all on account of you being The New Guy. You dropped a twenty on the bar, the bill glistening with fish blood. I knew you were trouble from just one look at that smile, but when's that ever stopped a gal from falling head over heels? I'm still falling.

"What'll it be?" I asked, trying not to notice your hazel eyes. Your slender lips hidden beneath that baleen of whiskers. We were really gonna have to do something about that beard.

"Whatever you're having."

"Club soda it is then."

"Make it a double."

You were just another itinerant fisherman coming in from North Carolina, South before that, Georgia before, slowly crawling your way up the coast, looking for work, following the fish.

"Name's Callum," you said.

"Jenny," I answered back.

I wondered how long you'd stay in town. If the risk of you disappearing was worth the heartbreak. I didn't want to wake one morning and realize you'd gone and vanished on me.

But you kept coming back to the bar. Even on your days off, you'd sit yourself down. Keep me company. You'd slip a quarter into the jukebox, always playing the same goddamn song.

Into the Mystic by Van Morrison. Lord, you were such a cheeseball.

It worked.

Some nights, those dead nights, you were my only customer. You'd help me close. How chivalrous, I thought. I'd wipe down the bar and you'd mop. I'd turn off the lights and we'd stay.

One drink occasionally became two.

Became three or four.

Why keep count?

"I don't think either of us is in any condition to drive home," I said as we stumbled out into the parking lot, met by nothing but black. Not a star in the sky.

There was the phone booth. Just standing out there in the dark. The sole sodium light suspended over the lot cast its dim glow over the booth's cracked glass, almost like a beacon.

"Hold up," you said as you moseyed over. "I'll call us a cab."

That made me laugh. "You know it doesn't work, right?"

"Says who?"

"Ma Bell."

"When's the last time you tried?"

You took my hand and dragged me into the booth with you. You wrestled against the door, its rusted hinges squealing as you sealed us in. I hadn't been this close to you before. The smell of you, the very brine of the bay, mixed in with whiskey. You reached into your pocket and fished out a quarter, holding it up to me between your fingers before slipping it into the slot.

Looked to me like you were performing some kind of magic trick. *Now you see it. . .*

"Wasting your money," I warned.

"Ye of little faith."

. . . Now you don't.

You picked up the phone and brought it to your ear. There simply wasn't any space between us. I was inhaling your exhales, dizzy with giddiness as you punched in a number.

Then silence.

You were listening, actually listening to. . .
whatever you were listening to. A dial tone? Was it
ringing? Did somebody answer? Was there someone on the other end of the line?

You held out the phone to me, this sober look
suddenly washing over your face.

"It's for you."

". . . Me?"

You nodded.

I held my breath as I took the phone out of your
hand and brought it up to my ear. For a moment—
just the briefest of heartbeats—I swear, I was ready
to believe someone was there.

On the other end of the line.

". . . Hello?"

Your lips cracked back into the shittiest shit-
eating grin and I knew, I knew you had me going.
You started laughing and I started laughing and
suddenly the windows were fogging up.

"See? Told you it worked. . ."

"Asshole." I hammered the phone over your
shoulder a few times, laughing my ass off.

"You just gotta *reach out and touch someone*. . ."

I dropped the phone and leaned forward and
my lips found yours as I forced you against the
glass, just to shut you up. Your whiskers were too
long and they slipped in my mouth, tickling my lips
like sea anemones fanning back and forth across a
coral alcove of your tongue.

Your beard was always in some sore need of trimming. We'd need to do something about that. Later. Not now, later. There were other things on my mind just now.

You wrapped your arms around my legs and lifted me up. My feet left the ground and I now found myself hoisted onto the metal ridge of the payphone, straddling you.

If anybody had been wandering through the marina's parking lot that night, they sure would've had themselves one hell of a show.

Nine months later, we welcomed Shelby into our lives.

You never left.

Brandywine—population 233—became your home.

234 now. I thought of you rooting yourself to us, just like that phone booth, a landline wired to the world, tethering you to this town. You weren't going nowhere.

You worked mornings and I worked nights. We did our handoffs at the marina. That was our routine. I'd always let Shelby play in the parking lot until you motored back in from the bay. We never had many customers during the day, so it was safe enough for her to kick the gravel around. I had a clear view through the window overlooking the wharf. She never left my sight.

A family of seagulls set up their nest along the booth's roof. The windows were painted in bird

shit, these white tear drops spackling the glass. For months, they'd just squat on top and watch the water, squawking away. You'd give Shelby a fish to feed the seagulls after you docked, teaching her to toss a herring straight into the air and watch the birds swoop in and swallow.

You were always more fun.

The better parent.

I'd spot her crawl in the booth and seal herself inside. I'd stop whatever I was doing and watch her talk on the phone. I never asked her who she was chatting to. Seemed private to me.

This was all before Aubrey took everything.

Took you.

Now I don't want our daughter getting anywhere near that fucking phone booth. I don't want her talking to nobody.

Least of all you.

Hurricane Aubrey was the first tropical cyclone of the year. She began brewing in the Bahamas, pounding Florida before climbing up the Carolinas, reaching Virginia with winds reaching ninety miles an hour and climbing. By the time she hit Brandywine, she was a category three hurricane.

Fifteen foot high storm surge wrecked most of the coast. Brandywine didn't stand much of a chance. All that overwash flattened out the sand dunes in seconds. Knocking out docks.

How many hurricanes had we seen together?

There was Bonnie the year before. Not to mention Floyd, barely a month after Shelby was born. Storms are a way of life around these parts. You just have to weather them *together*.

Nobody was leaving just because of some storm. Who cared what the governor said? That man could order everyone on the Chesapeake to head inland until he was blue in the face.

Where were we supposed to go? This is where we lived. This was our home. Your home.

So we put up plywood sheets. We nailed them to every last window.

We sealed ourselves in. *Batten down the hatches...*

We'd wait this storm out, just like all the others that had come before. There wasn't one hurricane, not one, that could tear our family apart. Our love was stronger than any storm, I thought. *Believed.* Our love was a force of nature in of itself, as elemental as wind and water.

"I'm just gonna check on the boat," you told me.

"Are you outta your goddamn mind?"

"I just need to make sure she's tied down."

"To hell with your boat," I said. "Listen to it out there." The winds had been picking up, shrill enough to sting my ears. Aubrey was at our doorstep, pounding her fists. She wanted in.

Wanted you.

I watched you slip out the door, like you were sneaking off to see some lady on the side. I found myself feeling jealous of some goddamn hurricane. Aubrey, The Other Woman.

"Be right back," you said. "Two shakes."

You never did.

The second Aubrey arrived in Brandywine, I reckoned the first thing she would've swatted away was that payphone, but for some bewildering reason, she blew right over it.

Spared it.

The seagulls were gone, their nest whisked away. But the booth was immovable. Rooted to the ground.

Let's not count the houses she knocked over. The roofs ripped right off their homes. Let's not talk about why she skipped over some stupid fucking phone booth and took you instead.

Twenty lives, all told. People I'd known all my life, taken. People I grew up with, gone.

You. You were no longer here.

Be right back, you said.

Your last words to me.

Most of me wishes they had found your body. But your disappearance made it easier for me to spin some black yarn to Shelby. Just another one of your homemade fairy tales. *Daddy got whisked out to sea, darling.* . . I wasn't nearly as good of a storyteller as you, but I did my best. You would've been proud.

Daddy's still out there, somewhere, swimming with the fishies...

Beats having to explain to our daughter what actually happened. How a gust of wind hit you at a hundred miles an hour. How it sent you right into the surge. How it dragged your body into the Chesapeake and then the ocean beyond, where the Coast Guard would never find you, bring you back, spinning your limbs in endless directions, grating your face over coral and sand.

You never trimmed that goddamn beard.

I missed your sea anemone whiskers.

You notice who's missing straight away. People you crossed paths with nearly every day are now no longer there. The aisles at the market are deserted. All the empty seats at the bar.

Felt like Brandywine was never growing back. Never going to heal.

All those houses. All those docks. All those people.

Now you see them...

Still had a phone booth, though. I resented it. Almost blamed that booth for losing you. All those memories of you and me, sealed inside its glass. A message in a bottle cast out to sea.

S

O

S

We had been told to move on with our lives. How does a town heal after losing so much? So many? Our governor swore up and down there'd be cleanup crews, that he'd fix the roads, rebuild our docks, but we still haven't seen one single cent of recovery funds. Not one single maintenance worker came down to Brandywine to survey the damage. Our damage.

No, we've had to clean up for ourselves.

To heal all on our own.

There were bikes in the trees, looking like rusted Christmas ornaments. Furniture strewn about the street. Couch cushions by the side of the road. Toys scattered in the battered corn fields. Clothes nobody would ever wear again now draped the telephone wires that hadn't miraculously snapped. The flotsam of our lives was still strung over miles of pummeled shore.

The very bones of who we were before.

Braddock's become a ghost bar inside a ghost town. I serve the survivors, but this sure didn't feel like surviving to me. Didn't feel like *life* anymore. The roof had ripped open. I had help patching it up. It wasn't the prettiest of repairs, but it'd suffice until the next hurricane.

Or the next.

I'd be lying if I didn't admit I found myself silently praying for a stray wind to sweep me away, too. Begging the next cyclone to take me with you. Wherever you were.

But there's Shelby to consider.

I keep finding her in the lot, looking out at the bay and I swear she's searching for you, wondering where you are. When will you swim back home? What am I supposed to tell her?

What can I say?

Be right back, you said.

You have no idea how pissed I'd been. How could you leave your daughter like that?

Leave me?

Be right back. That's all I ever heard anymore, echoing through my head. *Be right back...*

I wanted to give you a piece of my goddamn mind. To yell and shout and cry and—

Be right back...

Hear your voice. I wanted to hear your voice.

Be right back...

Just once more, that's all. I just wanted to talk to you one last time, that's it.

Be right back...

You promised.

Be right back...

I worked most days simply to keep myself busy. To occupy my thoughts with something other than you. Shelby would come and I'd simply cut her loose in the parking lot. There's no longer a dock for her to walk on. They all got washed away. She'd end up kicking the gravel around for hours, bored out of her mind, waiting for your trawler to pull in. Holding out hope.

That first week was an absolute blur. I couldn't tell you what happened right after Aubrey left. Those days are lost to me, even now. To all of us. Most of days I stared at the water.

Still do.

Folks swung by the bar. Just to be some place, any place, that felt close to normal. Like old times. We'd never been this busy before the storm, but now it's crammed full of people who don't talk. Don't drink. Don't do much of anything other than look out the bay window. Staring.

We're the ones Aubrey left behind.

Franklin Hull. Tammy Watkins. Carl Jessup. Henry Ketchum. Goodie Thomas. Some days there'd be more, some less, all of us huddled silently in our seats, simply staring out at the bay.

Waiting for the water to return what's ours.

"Ain't that Bekah?"

Can't remember who said it. Hell, it might've even been me. I couldn't recognize the sound of my own voice most days now, anyhow, so your guess is as good as mine.

We all turned to look out the bay window and sure enough, there's Bekah Brunstetler, standing in the phone booth. She'd lost her husband of forty three years, all thanks to Aubrey. Hank had been hit by a shingle that flew off their roof. Cracked his skull open right between his eyes. She was all alone now, wandering the streets in the same ratty bathrobe. I had to squint to make sure, but I'd be damned if she didn't have the receiver up to her ear, talking to somebody.

Talking.

I'm not one to pass judgement. We get through our grief however we can. Anything to make it through another day. Just one more. But I couldn't comprehend what Bekah was doing.

Who was she talking to?

When she was done, Bekah said *goodbye.* I was familiar enough with the shape your lips make when you say that word, blooming out on *good,* then curling and budding back out with *bye,* that I didn't need to hear it to know that's what she said. She hung the yellow phone back up on its receiver, pried open the shattered glass doors, and shuffled her way home again.

The very next day, Bekah came back.

And the next.

She'd stand out there for about an hour, holding the phone to her ear.

Chatting away.

The rest of us just watched her talk, lips moving, not hearing a single word she said. We all wondered out loud if she'd lost her goddamn mind. *Poor Bekah*, we said. Once she was done, she'd simply rest the phone back in its cradle and step out of the booth. Wander home again.

It wasn't until the fifth day that I finally mustered the gumption to ask her just what in the hell she was doing. I didn't want to—to, well,

interrupt her conversation, so I waited until she was done, struggling to pry herself out from the rusted doors and close them back up again.

"Bekah? You doing alright, hon?"

"Just fine." She definitely didn't look *just fine*. She hadn't run a comb through her hair in days, wearing the same damn natty bathrobe. She had on a pair of fuzzy slippers, all clumped in mud. Her right ear was flushed pink from pressing the phone against her lobe for too long.

But her eyes... I swear, there was a light inside. Burning bright.

I knew that look.

Hope.

"Why don't you come inside? Have a drink, on me." I placed a hand of her arm, ready to guide her back to the bar, but she resisted. Pulled free from me. She's stronger than I thought.

It took Bekah a moment to say anything, adrift in her mind, but when she did, her face brightened with this delirious giddiness that sent a chill through me. "He answered my call."

"... Who?"

"Hank."

Bekah came back every day. She slid into the booth. Picked up the phone. Brought it to her ear. And *talked*. We all watched her laugh, occasionally cry, as if someone was on the line.

On the other end. Talking back. Listening.

How many days do you think it took before the idea popped into my own head? How many times do you think I saw Bekah laugh and laugh before I wondered if I could laugh, too?

How long did it take me to gather the strength to try?

You'd laugh at me. I just knew you'd tease me for doing it. But I wanted to hear your voice again. I'd happily let you rag on my ass for hours on end if it meant hearing you jeer.

I knew it was silly. I knew I was being an absolute idiot. I didn't care. I simply did not give a rat's ass anymore. I needed to try. Just once. I waited until after closing time. I said goodbye to the last survivor, locking up behind them. I couldn't even call these people customers anymore. We're all just survivors, simply getting through the day so we can do it all over again tomorrow.

It was around eleven. Maybe midnight. The sun dropped long ago, the water nothing but a flat obsidian. There just wasn't anything to see out there now. No boats, no docks. Nothing.

The sodium lamp in the parking lot was the only source of light for miles. Most other street-lamps were still knocked down, leaving the water-front in darkness, but I knew it was there. The only thing lit up around here was the booth. A spotlight shining on that payphone.

I stepped forward. Then hesitated. When was the last time I actually slipped inside?

With you. Always you.

I had to force the door shut. It oddly felt bigger without you cramming in with me. The air was muggy, trapped behind the cracked glass. Even though most panes had been knocked out, it was still difficult for me to breathe in here. Shards of glass crumbled under my feet.

I couldn't believe I was doing this. Not that it stopped me. Bekah seemed so convinced, so sure of herself. The warmth in her eyes. The belief. How couldn't I try? Just once?

I lifted the scuffed yellow phone off the receiver, the plastic mouthpiece all chipped.

I held my breath. Brought it up.

And listened.

Ever hear the ocean when you press a shell against your ear? I didn't know what I was expecting, exactly. A wave crash of static. A dial tone. Or nothing. Just silence on the other end.

What I heard was you. Your voice.

. . . Jenny? That you?

I dropped the phone. More like my fingers loosened, the phone slipping out from my hand. The metal-coiled cable caught it, going taut right away and bouncing back up in the air in a hangman's rebound, where the body ricochets back up after its neck snaps around the noose.

I leapt back, away from the phone, hitting my head against the window behind me. I felt trapped all of a sudden, pinned behind a pane of glass. A butterfly staked in place, all framed.

The phone dangled on its wire, swaying like the pendulum on a grandfather clock.

There's no way, no possible way I heard—

Heard—

—you.

I quickly reached for the phone and brought it back to my ear, listening.

Jenny? Can you hear me? Are you there?

I barely had the breath inside of my lungs to say it, to muster up the single word—"Yes."

Thought I'd lost you there.

My knees softened. Legs gave out underneath me. I felt myself slide down the shattered glass wall until I slumped into this limp heap of limbs along the bottom of the booth.

I hadn't let go of the phone. I kept my grip, fingers tightening around the plastic handle. Its chipped mouthpiece so close to my lips. The receiver at my ear. "Is. . . is it really you?"

Your voice seeped through. *I knew you'd find me.*

Word got around quick. A town as small as Brandywine, it wouldn't take long for it to spread. Not everybody believed it at first, but most folks who'd lost someone were willing to try.

What did we have to lose that we hadn't lost already?

What was left?

— STAY ON THE LINE —

I remember seeing Franklin Hull, all eighty years of himself, slip inside that booth and seal himself in. Even from here, I could see his wrist tremble as he lifted the phone off the hook.

I saw Tammy Watkins talk to her son.

Carl Jessup spoke to his brother.

You always wanted to give people their privacy. This was their call. Their time to connect. You never wanted to ask who they'd been talking to. We didn't need to. We all knew.

This hurricane had taken so much, but Aubrey left us a miracle. A beacon.

The booth.

We set up a system. Rules for using the phone. No longer than thirty minutes at a time. Not a minute longer. You'd make your call and then it was someone else's turn. If you wanted to call back, you'd have to go to the end of the line and wait for your time to come up again.

And no telling anybody. No pictures. No social media posts. Nothing. This was just for us.

The survivors.

"You wouldn't believe how busy things are at the bar," I told you. "They're picking up."

I hadn't realized I was the one doing most of the talking. You didn't seem to mind. You listened as I filled you in on everything happening at Braddock's. In Brandywine. At home.

I filled the silence. There was far too much of that nowadays.

I miss it there. . . Miss you.

Your voice tickled my ear. Your words felt like the faintest filament brushing over the lobe. If I closed my eyes and concentrated, focused all my thoughts on you—the undertow of your voice—it almost felt like you were there, leaning over my shoulder, whispering into my ear.

Almost.

"Shelby drew a picture of you."

Oh? How do I look?

"Blue."

We'd talk for so long, my ear would sweat. I'd finally hang up and realize how sore my neck was, feeling that familiar crick from childhood, where my shoulder bones held up the phone. Remember way-back-when, the landline days, when we were still kids, when you talked to your friends on the phone, spending hours on end in bed just chatting away until well after bedtime and your parents finally told you to get off, hang up, and get some sleep, and there would be this kink in your neck and your ear would be so hot, still warm from the other person's voice? Remember? That's what this felt like to me. Like being a kid again, chatting on the phone.

Don't go. Please.

"I have to. . ."

Stay with me. Just a little longer. . .

"It's somebody else's turn, hon."

One more minute? Just one? Please? Your voice. . .

"I. . . I can't."

I need to hear your voice. It's all I have to hold on to. It's so lonely here. Your voice, your voice is all I've got. It's a lighthouse without the light. Your voice guides me home. . . I need it.

A lighthouse without the light.

A soundhouse, maybe?

A voicehouse?

The graffiti changed. For years, it had been nothing but lewd pictures and curse words. But somewhere along the way that vandalism was scrubbed off and replaced with the names of those we'd lost. That kudzu of Sharpie marker now luxuriated in a long-sprawling patch of loved ones, as if this phone booth were a memorial set up in an honor of those lost in the storm.

People repaired the broken widows. Someone swapped out the cracked glass for fresh panes. The hinges were oiled. The rust was scraped away. The metal frame polished until it shined.

Who, though?

I pulled into the lot one morning and wouldn't you know it, but somebody had brought in a couple terracotta pots full of fresh gardenias, lining them around the outside.

The booth's become a shrine.

A sanctuary.

We could speak to our loved ones. Reach out to them. Connect. Wherever they were, they were just on the other end of the phone. We just had to hold on to them. Stay on the line.

"Where are you?"

Here.

"But. . . where is here?"

With you. Your voice had the faintest crackle of static to it, as if we had a bad connection. You'd cut out for a breath and I'd feel my heart skip. I was afraid I'd lost you.

It was better not to ask so many questions. This is just the way things were. Aubrey whisked you away but the booth brought you back, some-how. Brought all of our people back.

What was the old AT&T commercial? How'd it go again? *Reach out and touch someone.*

I'd talk your ear off, if there wasn't a line forming outside. It was so hard to keep our calls within their designated time limit, just to be fair to one another. It was so hard to say goodbye.

Don't go. Not again.

"I'm sorry, I—"

Please, Jenny, you can't leave me again. . . I get so lonely when you're not here.

"I've got to give somebody else a turn. There's a line—"

Tell me about Shelby. Please? Tell me about our girl.

"She's doing okay. As okay as can be expected. There's a lot she doesn't understand." There was a hell of lot I didn't understand, either, to be completely honest. How's this possible?

I need to talk to her. . . Could you put her on the line?

Put her on the line. Something about the way you said it felt strange.

"Do you think that's a good idea?"

Why not?

"It's been hard enough trying to explain what happened. This might make things harder."

She's my daughter. . .

"I know, it's just—"

I need to speak with her. I need to hear her voice.

"I'll. . . I'll think about it."

Put her on. Please.

"I've got to go—"

Put her on the—

Nobody had seen Franklin Hull for a few days. I'm ashamed to admit this, but I hadn't even noticed. My mind was elsewhere. On you. In the booth.

When Franklin's body washed up on the shore, miles away from the payphone, we'd already gone through so much grief, there wasn't much left to give. His ears had been chewed off by crabs, the fish feasting on the soft parts of his flesh. It's unclear if he wandered into the water or if it'd been an accident, but all I can remember is the last time I saw him. In the booth.

He hung up the phone without saying goodbye. I watched him expel his frail frame from the folding doors and slowly wander through the lot. It didn't strike me as strange at the time, but instead of heading home, he slowly made his way toward the wharf. For the water.

I didn't give it much thought because it was finally my turn to—

reach out

—use the phone and I'd already been waiting for over an hour by then, so of course I didn't want to waste another second. Not another breath.

There you are.

"I'm here."

I was worried you'd forgotten about me...

"How could I forget you?"

Stay. Stay with me. Please.

"I'm here. I'm not going any—"

Just stay on the line.

Shelby finally asked about you one night while I was tucking her in. "Is it true?"

"What's that, hon?"

"You're talking to Daddy?"

Something about her question caught me off guard. I wasn't ready to tell her. What was I supposed to say? Yes, yes, hon, your father is on the phone right now. He's always on the line...

Just waiting for us to pick up. Answer his call. Why couldn't I tell her?

I'm steering her clear of the booth. I can't explain why, but there was a part of me that still felt uncertain about it all. Maybe I was just being selfish. Maybe I wanted you all to myself.

Is that awful of me? Depriving our daughter of hearing your voice?

Put her on the line, you said. It didn't sound like you meant the phone.

It felt more like a hook.

A fishing hook.

Tammy Watkins vanished a couple days later. Same thing. She took her call. Went over her time limit. When she finally hung up, the blank expression on her face was hard to read.

"You okay, Tammy?"

She never said. She hasn't been back to the bar since.

Nobody's found her body yet.

"Shelby's birthday is coming up," I told you. "This one'll be hard. Her first without you."

How old's she again?

"She's turning five."

Five, right.

It was easy to forgive you if you got some facts wrong. You made mistakes. Misremembered certain things, simple things, easy to correct and move on with our talks.

Why hadn't you remembered your own mother's name?

How could you forget the name of the bar?

How could you forget your daughter's birthday?

It didn't matter. None of that mattered. Not really. I chalked it all up to the fact that you were... wherever you were. It was bound to be hard to remember every last little thing.

I knew I just needed to hold on to you however I could.

Keep you on the line.

On the line. Jesus, it even sounds like you were some kind of fish, not some voice on the phone. *Just stay on the line*, I thought to myself. Prayed every time I picked up the phone.

Just stay on the line...

The line only got longer the more word spread about the booth, which meant the wait for our turn stretched on, too. Carl Jessup kept growing more impatient, kicking gravel in the lot.

"That was longer than thirty minutes," he muttered to me as I stepped out.

"Sorry?"

"It's my turn." I notice how red his ear was. Infected, almost. A fiery coral complexion, bruised and blistered from too much chafing.

I followed Carl after he finished his phone call. Just to see where he went. I kept my distance, unsure if I should intervene when I watched him wander onto what remained of his own dock, this rickety old thing barely holding itself up by its barnacle-covered posts. He kept walking toward the end, never stopping. Not once. His focus was on the water. On his brother.

I shouted out his name the second his foot stepped off and he—

crrsh

—dropped right into the water. By the time I reached the shore, he was gone.

Our calls were changing us. Crossing our wires, somehow.

Crossed lines.

We all had people we wanted—*needed*—to speak to. People on the other side. All you had to do was slide the door closed, pick up the phone, answer the call, and there they'd be.

Their voice.

But something was wrong. This didn't feel right anymore. You didn't feel right.

I need to talk to Shelby. I need to hear her voice. Put her on the line.

People are making their pilgrimage to the payphone now.

New people.

Word got out somehow. I don't know how it spread, but news of the booth has gone beyond Brandywine. The lot is always full. I've told Shelby she can't play out there anymore on account of the cars. So many strangers. I don't recognize their faces. These people came to—

reach out

—communicate with the other side. It's no longer only our loved ones. Not just the people Hurricane Aubrey took from Brandywine. It's everybody, *anybody* who's passed on. It doesn't matter where they died or how. The phone booth is for anyone who wants to—

touch someone

—put in a collect call to the afterlife. Business has never been better, if I'm being honest. The bar is alive. Thriving. Brandywine is becoming a town again. Almost feels like home.

Isn't that what I wanted? You gave this to me. This was your gift.

Bekah Brunstetler's body had been submerged underwater for so long, it was practically impossible to identify her beyond the strips of her bathrobe draped over her bones, most of the meat pecked clean by the crabs. She'd been the first to answer the call. Look where it got her.

It's time, you said. *I want you to join me. Come to me.*

"Where?"

Here.

"How?"

It's so easy. . . All you have to do is follow the sound of my voice.

"What about Shelby?"

She can come too. . .

"Callum, I. . . I'm sorry. I can't do this anymore."

Then put someone else on the line. Put Shelby on. Let me speak to her.

I couldn't help but notice the change in your voice.

"No."

A wave of static crashed over my ear. *PUT HER ON THE LINE.*

There was sand in your mouth. Stones in your throat. Rocks between your teeth.

It didn't sound like you at all.

It wasn't, was it?

You?

A hand smacked the window just at my face, startling me. I dropped the phone. I let out a shout, spinning around to see the desperate face of a stranger just outside the booth. His nose was practically pressed against the glass, his breath fogging up the window. He hammered his open palm flat against the outside of the booth once more, slapping the glass, eager to get in.

"My turn," he muttered. Whoever he was. His ear looked chafed. Inflamed.

I hear the ocean wherever I go now, even when I'm not on the phone. It's this slight hiss of static always at the back of my head. A white noise machine. Crashing waves in my skull.

Your voice. I don't even need to be on the line to hear you now.

You're in my head.

I had a nightmare about you. We were on the phone together, talking for what felt like hours. Maybe even days. Who can tell anymore? It must've been night because it was completely dark outside. I'd lost track of time again. Where had the day gone?

There was something strange about the darkness beyond the booth. It was murky. Green, almost. I leaned forward and squinted, trying to get a better look at what was on the other side of the glass.

Water. It was the ocean. The booth was now submerged at the bottom of the bay.

"Do you see—" I started to ask you, but cut myself off.

See what? You asked. *What do you see?*

There was the slightest tickle at my ear.

I yanked back the phone.

Gasped.

There. *Right there.* Roots reaching out of the receiver. Tiny red buds rose up from the colander of holes in the mouthpiece. Every last one had the thinnest living rivulet. Reminded me of a Play-Doh Fun Factory, the colored clay seeping through. All these splurging worms. Tendrils fanned out from the phone, reaching for my ear. My mouth. They wanted to come in.

See what, Jenny? The tendrils trembled with the sound of your voice, vibrating like living guitar strings, as if they were your own vocal cords. *What do you see, Jenny?*

If I opened the door, the ocean would flood the booth. I was trapped as the roots wrapped around the wrist of my hand still holding the phone, lacing their way up my arm.

They found my throat.

Choking me.

If my lips split to scream, the tendrils would slip into my mouth. I had to keep my lips sealed, *batten down the hatches*, and hold the phone as far away from me as possible.

I can't breathe...

The tendrils kept coming, pouring freely from the phone. A latticework of angry red roots wove over my chest. I could feel them working towards my ears. My nose. Any way in.

I can't breathe...

I had to snap it off at the source. Cut off your voice. I tugged on the phone, pulling so hard. The cord gave, but instead of breaking, it stretched— stretched beyond the coiled cable, beyond its wires, melding into a red stem that tugged back on itself, pulsing under the dim light.

I can't breathe...

The roots cinched tighter around my throat. The oxygen in my lungs burned. A constellation of black spots scattered across my eyes. I kept yanking on the phone, suddenly playing tug-of-war with the booth. Hand over hand, I pulled and pulled on its pulsating cable, but that stem kept coming, unspooling from within, falling into a livid, wriggling heap at my feet.

I can't...

I knew I was fading. I couldn't hold out much longer. The root in my hands had the same fleshy consistency as a tongue, wet and pink. Not a tongue. A sea anemone. Something from the bottom of the ocean. Something stirred up by the storm. *Reaching* out for me. *Touching* me.

I...

Just as I was about to black out, just as all the ink spots in my eyes nearly eclipsed my vision, those roots noosed around my neck, squeezing so tight I had no choice but to open my mouth and gasp for air, letting them in, letting them all in, a tiny hand—a child's hand—smashed against the glass.

Shelby.

Shelby, my baby girl. She was on the other side of the window. Outside the booth. In the ocean. She floated through the water, her feet off the ground, hair fanning as if it were kelp.

Her father must've finally found her, I thought.

You took her from me.

Shelby grabbed hold of the folding metal door and pulled. A spate of water spilled through the crack in the phone booth's door, the surge growing the more she tugged. I barely had the strength to

push the door shut. The booth was flooding. My baby girl was coming in.

When Shelby's lips lifted into a grin I couldn't recognize, her own mother, the same sea anemones slipped over her lips, a dozen different tongues branching out from her mouth. They wormed their way over the glass until it cracked, winnowing through the fresh fractures.

I saw the sea anemones reach out from her eyes and touch me—

When I woke up with a start, letting out a shout in bed, in my own home, the dream wasn't what terrified me. What scared me the most was the sudden compulsion to call you.

Tell you what happened.

Teens gather in the lot. Not coming into the bar, simply hanging out. Waiting their turn. It's become a dare. A thing to prove. Kids come from all around, mustering the courage to pick up the phone. Answer the call. They'll simply stand there and tilt their heads back, listening to the sea. The ocean crash of static on the other end of the line, rushing right into their ears.

Whose voice is on the other end of the line for them, I wonder. Who have they lost? Maybe it doesn't matter. What if it's been the same person on the other side, calling us all?

What if you just want to keep us all on the line?

Here's what I think: it was never our loved ones. Never the ones we lost.

It was just you. Only you. Whoever—
whatever
—you are.

You've been feeding off our grief. And when we're empty, you sever ties—cut the line—and let us go, what's left of us at least, catch and release, back into the water where we drown.

It was never my Callum.

It was you.

You.

I caught Shelby in the booth today. I was behind the bar, losing myself to the water beyond the window, when I glanced at the payphone and spotted her. So small. Her head barely reached the number pad on the phone. She had the receiver up to her ear. I couldn't hear what she was saying, but I saw her lips split into that grin I'd never seen before. Only in my dreams.

I ran for the booth. Ran so fast. When I reached the folding doors, I yanked them open. Shelby gave a start, nearly dropping the phone. Her back pressed against the glass.

"I told you," I shouted as I grabbed the phone right out from her hand and slammed it back on the receiver. "You can't be in here. I don't want you ever, *ever*, in here."

Shelby shrieked at me and didn't stop, this endless peal of a scream reaching out from her throat. It didn't sound like her, barely sounded human, and oh God, for the life of me, I couldn't make her stop. No matter how hard I shook her, trying to snap her out of it, she kept on screaming and screaming, "I was talking to Daddy I was talking to Daddy I was talking to Dad—"

You can't have her. Shelby's not yours.

Please. Not her.

I waited until the crowd had thinned out for the day. Bound to be around midnight. Maybe later. The only illumination was the sodium light overhead, casting its dull beam over the booth. Once I knew no one else was around, I crept back into the booth. Sealed the glass door.

I lifted the phone off the receiver one last time. How couldn't I? I brought it to my ear. I didn't say anything. I just held my breath and waited for you to answer.

Jenny? That you?

I asked straight away: "Who are you?"

It's me. . . Who else would it be?

"Who are you?"

The line went dead for a second. Then you started to laugh. It was a husky chuckle, unfamiliar to me, but you kept on laughing, the volume only growing louder. Harsher.

Whoever you want me to be. . .

It wasn't your voice anymore. All that sand and sediment scraping over your throat. The awful sound of it filled the booth, so loud, flooding the suffocating space until I was drowning.

There was water at my feet. So cold. I could feel the surface rising up my legs, my hips.

I couldn't escape the booth. I kept pounding against the glass with the phone, but it wouldn't shatter. Your voice kept rising up my waist, reaching my chest, my throat. . . my mouth.

How long have you been feeding off our grief? Feeding off me?

reaching

out

touching

some

one

I cricked my neck back and took one last gasp of air before the water rose over my head.

I wrapped the coiled wire around my hand and made a fist.

I pulled as hard as I could.

Yanked on the cable until the phone finally snapped free.

The doors to the booth finally yawned opened on their own. I burst out and gasped for fresh air on a wave of expelled seawater, washing over the lot, taking the phone with me.

The cable was still wrapped around my fist. The wire dug into my skin.

. . . Jenny? You still there?

I ran to the edge of the marina, overlooking the bay. It was far too dark to see the water, but I heard it. The ocean. Its sibilant hiss, like a bad connection.

— STAY ON THE LINE —

Just stay on the line, Jenny, just stay on the—
I threw the phone as hard as I could but I never heard it splash.

The following morning, the first people to stand in line for the phone are going to find what's left of the booth, now smashed and toppled on its side, its glass shattered, the folding door crushed under the front of my car. I'll be behind the wheel, staring out at the Chesapeake.

Just waiting for you to call me back.

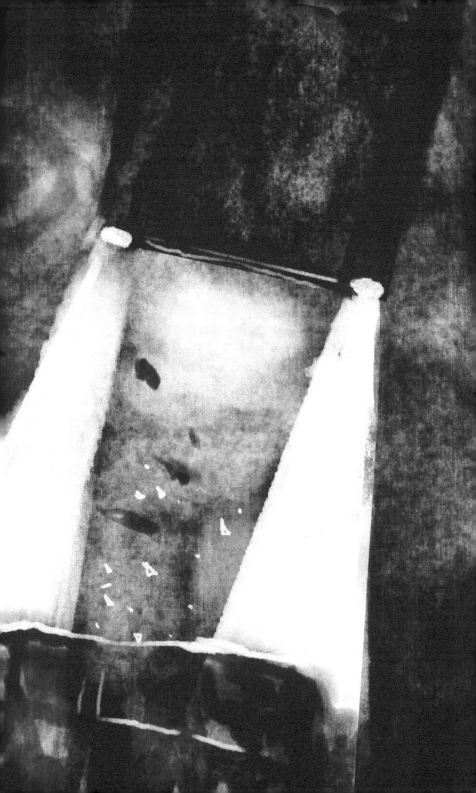

— ACKNOWLEDGMENTS —

Thank you, Trevor.
Thank you, Alan and the Shortwave family.

Thank you, Nick McCabe at The Gotham Group.
Thank you, Judith Karfiol.

Thank you, Lauren Gennawey and
Broken Road Productions.

Thank you, Jhanteigh Kupihea, Rebecca
Gyllenhaal and everyone at Quirk Books.

Thank you, Jasper and Cormac.
Thank you, Indrani.

Thank you for picking this up.

— ABOUT THE AUTHOR —

Clay McLeod Chapman writes books, comic books, children's book, and for film/TV. He is the author of the novels *What Kind of Mother, Ghost Eaters, Whisper Down the Lane, The Remaking,* and *miss corpus.*

claymcleodchapman.com

— ABOUT THE ILLUSTRATOR —

Trevor Henderson is a Toronto-based illustrator and writer. He most recently wrote and illustrated the middle-grade horror book *Scarewaves* for Scholastic. His love of monsters, cryptids, ghosts and other horrible entities is enduring and vast. Whenever he is not drawing or writing horrible things, he is probably playing with his cat Boo.

— ABOUT THE PUBLISHER —

Shortwave Publishing is an independent small press based in the Pacific Northwest. Shortwave offers a selection of original books, zines, and magazine stories with a focus on dark and speculative genre fiction.

View their full catalog at shortwavepublishing.com

— ALSO AVAILABLE —

THE
CHAPMAN CHAPBOOK
COLLECTION

"Mama Bird" is the dark and unsettling tale of a young picky eater and the mother willing to do anything to feed her child.

"Baby Carrots" is the story of a man haunted by a bad batch of produce.

"Knockoffs" are popping up everywhere. Online, on vacation, and—soon—on your block!

—

Each issue of the Chapman Chapbook series features a complete, standalone short story. The first 100 copies of each issue are hand-signed and numbered by the author.

Available exclusively in the Shortwave Shop.

shop.shortwavepublishing.com

— ALSO AVAILABLE —

MORE STORIES BY
CLAY McLEOD CHAPMAN
IN SHORTWAVE ANTHOLOGIES

OBSOLESCENCE: A Dark Sci-Fi, Fantasy, and Horror Anthology

Edited by Alan Lastufka and Kristina Horner

27 Brand-New Tales of Technological Terror, including Chapman's "pump and dump", alongside new stories by Adam Cesare, Gabino Iglesias, Ai Jiang, Eric LaRocca, Tanya Pell, Hailey Piper, and more.

—

Shadows in the Stacks: A Horror Anthology

Edited by Vincent V. Cava, James Sabata, and Jared Sage

This charity anthology includes Chapman's **"nathan ballingrud's haunting horror recs"**, alongside new stories by Jamie Flanagan, Jonathon Maberry, J.A.W. McCarthy, Tim McGregor, and more.

— ALSO AVAILABLE —

KILLER VHS SERIES
"The modern day Goosebumps for adults." — Horror Obsessive

Melon Head Mayhem
Alex Ebenstein

Cousins Carson and Sophia are in town for their grandma's funeral. They discover an old unfamiliar VHS tape that summons movie monsters—local urban legends called melon heads—into their very real lives!

—

Candy Cain Kills
Brian McAuley

When Austin's parents drag him and his little sister Fiona to a remote cottage for Christmas, he's less than thrilled about the forced bonding exercise. But after learning that their holiday getaway was the site of a horrific crime, this family on the rocks will have to fight for their lives against a legendary killer... because Candy Cain is slashing through the snow with a very long naughty list.

Milton Keynes UK
Ingram Content Group UK Ltd.
UKHW040237301024
450244UK00001B/3